I0596786

She had loved him, and he betrayed her, so now it was time to move on…

Amy wasn't pregnant. She sobbed about that for days. She'd pathetically hoped to keep some part of him.

Liz and her parents hovered in and out of her apartment in Petoskey, near Lake Michigan where she worked as marketing manager for a resort. She'd planned to let the lease expire next month after she moved into Gray's condo in Traverse City after her intimate June wedding. Gray had started a business with Luke building cottage and resort properties when they got back from Afghanistan.

He had told her they would honeymoon in Paris, but wouldn't divulge any details because he said he wanted to surprise her.

Andrew, her boss at her resort, had been a guest at the wedding and was very understanding. She looked at her passport she'd been so afraid wouldn't come in time. Gray had laughed and told her not to stress. She looked at her wistful expression in the passport photo.

Fuck this.

She called Liz, and they purged her apartment of everything he had given her, touched, or even looked at in a bonfire at Liz's parents' place on Lake Michigan.

Then Amy got back to work.

He loves her, but he can never forgive her for what she did to his friend…

Grayson Reardon blames Amy McDonald for the death of his friend, Smitty, who was killed on patrol in Afghanistan just after Amy broke up with him via Skype. Gray has always loved Amy but stayed away because Smitty saw her first. In an attempt to avenge his friend, Gray tricks Amy into accepting his marriage proposal and then dumps her at the altar, humiliating her in front of her family and friends. But Gray is torn between his love for Amy and his loyalty to Smitty, especially since Smitty's tall tales about his relationship with Amy don't quite mesh with reality, and—now that it's too late—Gray begins to realize he's made a terrible mistake.

She loves him, but he betrayed her, and she's determined to move on…somehow.

Amy has always loved Gray and broke up with Smitty because of it. But she feels guilty for what happened to him, so even though she learns what Gray has planned, she goes through with it, allowing him to publicly humiliate her. Now that it's over, and he's had his revenge, she's convinced Gray hates her. Determined to purge him out of her life forever, she throws away every reminder of

him and concentrates on her work. She almost suc-
ceeds—until fate intervenes, and Amy discovers that
things aren't always what they seem…

friends by calling it off minutes before their vows are said. Amy is devastated when he leaves her at the altar and vows to forget she ever knew him. Gray, on the other hand, realizes he's made a terrible mistake and lost the woman he truly loves, but how can he get her back? Cabin Fever is cute, fun, charming, and hot. The characters are well developed, the plot filled with surprises, and the sex scenes hot and plentiful. I enjoyed it very much. ~ *Regan Murphy, The Review Team of Taylor Jones & Regan Murphy*

ACKNOWLEDGMENTS

To the awesome members of the Greater Detroit Romance Writers of America for all the support and encouragement.

To the staff and other writers at Black Opal Books.

To my husband and family for…well, everything.

ALSO BY

TARA ELDANA

Reclaiming Lexi

Under the Riptides

Double Dare

In the Depths

On Thin Ice

Cabin Fever

Tara Eldana

A Black Opal Books Publication

GENRE: STEAMY ROMANCE/CHICK LIT/WOMEN'S FICTION

This is a work of fiction. Names, places, characters and incidents are either the product of the author's imagination or are used fictitiously, and any resemblance to any actual persons, living or dead, businesses, organizations, events or locales is entirely coincidental. All trademarks, service marks, registered trademarks, and registered service marks are the property of their respective owners and are used herein for identification purposes only. The publisher does not have any control over or assume any responsibility for author or third-party websites or their contents.

DEDICATION

For everybody who believes in second chances.

Chapter 1

He'd done it.

Amy was with her bridesmaids, waiting to marry him.

All he, Grayson, had to do was walk out and call it off like he'd planned.

She'd dumped Smitty, his best friend, on a Skype call while he and Smitty were serving a tour in Afghanistan. Then Smitty got killed, likely from being distracted at having his heart ripped out of his body.

"You good, man?" said Luke, his best man.

Gray and Luke were best friends and partners. They built condos and commercial buildings near Lake Michigan. He and Luke had been in Smitty's platoon.

"You got cold feet about dumping her ass?"

"No," Gray said. He pulled on his collar. His blood ran cold in his veins, like it had before he led his own platoon out on patrol in the mountains of Afghanistan. He set his mouth in a grim line.

Think of Smitty, not her.

"Let's do this," Luke said.

Gray nodded. "Let's go."

୧୬୧୬

Liz, Amy's maid of honor, held Amy's veil back while Amy expelled the contents of her stomach into the toilet. She took long, deep breaths.

"I think I'm good, Liz," she said.

"Bullshit," Liz hissed. "You're so not good, Ames. You're pregnant, aren't you?"

Amy sipped the glass of water Liz handed her, trying not to smudge her lipstick.

"It was just one time. That doesn't happen, does it? It has to be nerves," Amy said.

"Just one time?" Liz yelled. "Are you fucking kidding me? You've only done it with the guy you're going to marry just one time?" She took both of Amy's hands and held them. "Something's not right about him, about this. Why so fast? You've only been dating for six months. No guy proposes that fast. Did he ask you right after?"

"No," Amy said. "And I seduced him. And that was only three weeks ago. I've been in love with him forever, even when I was with Smitty, but he never even looked at me. That's why I broke it off with Smitty. I wanted to feel that for the man I married. There was nothing going on between me and Gray ever, not until after."

"You didn't tell him you still had your V-card, did you?" Liz said.

"He was surprised, shocked really," Amy said.

"Holy hell."

"Liz, I'm going to puke." Amy raced for the toilet, but nothing came up. "I'm okay."

"I'm going to get you some ginger ale," Liz said.

☙❧☙

Gray looked across the meadow where a handful of his and Amy's friends and family waited for them to declare their undying love for each other. He'd hustled her to agree to a small wedding.

He pulled hard on the collar of his dress shirt and tux. It felt like it was strangling him.

She was a virgin.

It didn't make sense.

Smitty described Amy and what they'd supposedly done in excruciating detail.

It was all typical Smitty bullshit.

Gray had incontrovertible proof. What else had Smitty lied about?

Amy was so tight his dick got hard remembering it. He'd made her come repeatedly with his hands and his mouth. She was so responsive, and she seemed so surprised by her reaction to him.

He told her he wanted them to be married before he sank himself inside her, but the truth was he couldn't stomach the thought that she had given that to Smitty first.

But she hadn't.

Her small, soft hands on his body made him insane with wanting her, like he'd always wanted her, even when she was with Smitty. Gray had even moaned her name when he was with more than one of the nameless women he'd fucked in college.

That night she was so determined to seduce him.

The little vixen impaled herself on him and cried out when he'd breached her hymen. After that, he was lost. He couldn't stop. He rode her hard, and she screamed his name. He spilled his seed inside her, and she milked his cock dry. He hadn't had protection because he was determined to resist her, and he had until that night.

He'd carried her to the shower and gently cleaned her. Then he settled her in his arms in bed. She called his name, reached for his dick, and said she loved him, all in a deep sleep.

She loved him.

She told Smitty she loved him, too.

She was a heartless bitch. She had to be.

Gray forced himself to remember his friend in the body bag they'd shipped him home in.

Smitty was a lieutenant. Two weeks after Amy broke up with him, he led his platoon on patrol into a remote area and got ambushed. Smitty would not have been so careless if Amy hadn't fucked with his head. At least he was the only casualty from his platoon.

The bitch had to pay.

"The car's ready," Luke said. "You going to wait till she walks up there to dump her, right?"

Grayson nodded. He felt sick to his soul. He didn't see Liz behind them.

♋♋

"Fuck," Liz yelled. She threw the can of ginger ale across the room. Amy's mother, Nancy had just left.

"What?" Amy picked up her bouquet of pink hydrangeas. She checked the mirror. Her blonde hair was arranged under the veil so the back hung down in curls. Her brown eyeliner and mascara made her eyes look bluer, and she touched up her blush so she didn't look so pale.

"I heard them, Ames. That prick Luke said the car's ready and asked Gray if he was going to wait till you walked up there to dump you."

Amy swayed on her feet. "It was too good to be true," she whispered. "I just wanted it to be."

Liz grabbed hold of her.

"He hates me for what happened to Smitty," Amy said. "I thought, I hoped, he was just grieving. He would never talk about it. I tried to explain. I hate me for what I did to Smitty. I deserve this." Tears streamed down her cheeks. "I should have done it before his reserve unit got called up. But it happened so fast. There was no good time."

Liz sobbed. "It's not your fault, any of it," she said. Her brown eyes blazed with anger.

"It is," Amy said. "All of it. Karma. Let's get this over with."

Maybe then she could forget Gray and move on. Her part in Smitty's death would always be with her. Gray's public hatred of her might help her guilt and sorrow dissolve, or Gray's sorrow anyway.

"You can't be serious," Liz said. "Why would you let him do this to you? Just leave now."

Amy shook her head. "He left so fast after our night together," she said. "He said there was a problem on a project in Indiana he had to sort out."

He'd come back just three days ago. To do this.

She took her father Steve's arm while Liz sobbed. Amy's mother asked Liz three times if she was okay and looked at Amy in concern. Liz stared hard at Amy.

"He loves you, Amy," Nancy said. "I've seen the way he looks at you when he thinks nobody's watching." She kissed Amy on her cheek and walked up the aisle on Luke's arm.

Liz seethed then sauntered up the aisle, not waiting for him to escort her, as they had practiced.

Amy nodded at Liz when she took her place next to Gray and Luke. Amy's father cupped her cheek.

"Amester, are you sure? You and Liz seem upset. And Gray looks like he's about to pass out. Is something wrong?"

Amy looked at Gray. He'd tamed his wavy, dark brown hair, and his hard jawline was clean shaven. He watched her, unsmiling. Amy clutched her father's arm and nodded.

Game on.

She walked on her father's arm to where they stood

next to the minister. Liz continued to sob, and the guests looked concerned.

Gray's hazel eyes looked glassy as Amy drew closer and closer. Her dad kissed her cheek then left her.

Amy looked at Gray, probably for the last time in her life.

"I always loved you," she whispered, smiling through her tears before she faced the minister.

Chapter 2

Gray felt his soul and heart detach from his body as he said the words he'd rehearsed so many times. Gasps went through the crowd. She'd looked at him fearlessly when her father handed her into his care, as if she knew what he was going to do. She said she always loved him, always him.

Smitty said something about how she told him she loved someone else, and it wasn't fair to him—that he, Smitty, deserved someone who loved him that way.

Gray turned his back on the woman who gave her virginity to him and left with Luke.

Smitty lied.

So why had Gray gone through with this half-assed plan to avenge Smitty after she gave him her virginity and said she loved him always, even knowing he planned to humiliate her in front of everyone she cared about?

Luke drove, spewing garbage about Amy until Gray told him to shut the fuck up.

❦❦❦

Amy wasn't pregnant. She sobbed about that for days. She'd pathetically hoped to keep some part of him.

Liz and her parents hovered in and out of her apartment in Petoskey, near Lake Michigan where she worked as marketing manager for a resort. She'd planned to let the lease expire next month after she moved into Gray's condo in Traverse City after her intimate June wedding. Gray had started a business with Luke building cottage and resort properties when they got back from Afghanistan.

He had told her they would honeymoon in Paris, but wouldn't divulge any details because he said he wanted to surprise her.

Andrew, her boss at her resort, had been a guest at the wedding and was very understanding. She looked at her passport she'd been so afraid wouldn't come in time.

Gray had laughed and told her not to stress. She looked at her wistful expression in the passport photo.

Fuck this.

She called Liz, and they purged her apartment of everything he had given her, touched, or even looked at in a bonfire at Liz's parents' place on Lake Michigan.

Then Amy got back to work.

☙☙☙

Gray tried to read through the requests for proposals from developers and cities asking for bids on construction projects, but all he could think of was Amy. She fearlessly faced him in her wedding dress as if she knew what he planned. She was so damn beautiful and brave.

She had been so sweet and loving when he pursued her. Their friends and family said it was a whirl-wind romance. They'd known each other since they were sophomores at Michigan State.

But Smitty saw her first.

Gray, Smitty, and Luke joined the Marine Corps Reserves to pay off their student loans. Their unit was called up two months after they graduated, so they went in as officers. Nothing prepared them for guerilla warfare and the unspeakable brutality.

And Amy fucking broke up with Smitty on Skype at

Camp Leatherneck in Afghanistan just before they were going to ship out.

Gray was in the room when she did it. She sobbed and said it wasn't fair to Smitty to lead him on, that she wanted him to be free when he came home to find someone who loved him and wanted him like he deserved. Then Smitty got orders to lead his platoon out on patrol one last time.

Why had Smitty lied about the stuff he'd said he and Amy did together? It had twisted Gray's guts to hear him talk that shit. He thought of all those sweet, shy smiles she had given him when he caught her staring at him before she dropped her eyes. Was she trying to see if he felt anything for her?

He'd fucked his share of women in college. But he realized it was her sweet angel face he saw whenever he found his release.

He remembered how she went down on him, how she screamed his name when he made her come.

If she was his, he'd never talk shit about her to another guy.

She was his, dammit.

And he'd fucked it up.

He hadn't looked at or touched another woman since he left her standing next to the minister.

He had to get out of his office before he smashed it to pieces.

"Hey, buddy." Luke walked into Gray's office. "Did you look over the RFPs?"

"No," Gray said. He stood up. "I'm taking some time at the cabin near Munising."

"Lake Superior is still cold, Gray. Stay here."

"No," Gray yelled. "Deal."

⌘

Two months later, Amy sat at her desk, scanning the inbox of her email.

What did she expect, an e-apology from Gray, an avowal of his undying love?

She saw one from Liz.

Tonight. Your place. I mean it. I'll bring wine. Lots of it.

Liz was persistent.

Amy stayed busy returning sales calls. She also handled marketing for the catering side of the hotel's business.

Catering comprised eight percent of the business of Paradise on the Bay's highly rated restaurant and the conference center, onsite and offsite.

She'd solely focused on her job after it happened.

She'd rebuffed all Liz's offers to set her up and ignored interested smiles from men.

She felt frozen.

೧೧೧

Liz and Amy were into their second bottle of Merlot. They'd scarfed down one cheese and sausage pizza when someone knocked on the door of Amy's apartment.

She looked suspiciously at Liz who threw her hands in the air.

"I didn't invite anyone, I promise." Liz looked out Amy's peephole.

"Fuck."

"What?" Amy said.

"It's ass wipe Luke." Liz grabbed her purse. She carried a 22-caliber handgun, and she knew how to shoot it. Her dad and brothers were county sheriffs. Liz pulled the gun out of her purse and hid it behind her.

"Is that thing loaded?" Amy whispered.

"Of course it's loaded," Liz hissed. "You don't carry a gun unless it's loaded. I've told you this before. Open the door. Let the ass wipe in. I've got the safety on, for now."

Amy looked the peephole. Luke ran his fingers through his brown hair. He looked agitated. He had dark circles under his eyes and a scruffy beard.

She swung her door open halfway. "What do you want?"

"Can we do this inside?"

She let him in.

"You look like shit," Liz said.

He gasped when he saw the gun she aimed at him.

"You have two minutes, ass wipe. You will not hurt her again."

"Liz, take it easy," Amy said. "What do you want?"

"For fuck's sake, lower that thing," he said. "You think I'd be here if there was anything else I could do?"

"Lower it, Liz," Amy said.

Liz did, reluctantly.

Luke sighed. "It's Gray."

"What does that have to do with me?"

"He's bad, Amy. Our business is going to shit.'

"I don't care."

"He's been holed up in the cabin on Lake Superior for two months. In summer, our busiest time."

Liz advanced on him holding her 22, but not pointing it at him. "What does she care if the jack wipe is taking a vacation?' she sneered.

"He's drinking all day, every day," Luke said.

Holy hell.

Gray's dad was an Alcoholics Anonymous sponsor,

and Gray barely drank, not even in college.

She would not let herself care. "It's not my problem," she said.

"He barely eats and when he's out of it—" He hesitated and bit his lip. "—he calls your name, Amy."

"Liar," she screamed.

"I'm not," Luke said.

She clenched her hands into fists so tight she felt her fingernails break the skin. "Everything he did or said to me was a lie. So is this."

"Get out," Liz said.

"I don't give a shit about the business," he said. "This is about Gray. Could you just go and—"

"No," she said. "I won't."

"For Smitty, please?" he said.

Amy sucked in her breath.

"You shit," Liz said, aiming her gun. "Get out," she hissed.

He left, and Amy collapsed onto her ottoman.

Luke was right.

She owed Smitty.

Chapter 3

Amy texted Liz that she'd arrived at Gray's cabin. She saw his Harley parked at the back of the property and listened to the waves of Lake Superior lapping the rocky shore. The sun blazed hot. It would stay light a long time in late August, after ten at night because of how far north it was and how close they were to the Central Time Zone.

Was he near the water? She left her purse and keys in her car with her windows down and picked her way toward the rocky beach. It was wilder there than it was near Lake Michigan. This deep lake had frozen completely for the last two winters, much like Amy's heart had when

Gray turned his back on her on their phony wedding day.

An old rowboat was tipped upside down on the shore. He was nowhere she could see. She had to go inside.

Damn you, Smitty.

He'd persuaded her to stay at a stupid frat party she was going to ditch by pulling a quarter out of her ear. He made her laugh with his lopsided grin and droll humor.

He had lively blue eyes, dark blond hair, and a lean build—nothing like his best friend Gray Reardon, who had wavy brown hair and intense brown eyes, tiger eyes that never held hers for more than a couple seconds.

She felt shivery whenever he was close to her, despite the fact she never saw him with the same girl twice. Smitty shared an apartment with him and said he fucked around a lot. She loved Smitty, but when he kissed her or held her, it was Gray she thought of.

So she put Smitty off when he wanted sex, hoping she would come to want him the way she wanted Gray.

That never happened.

She made her way to the back door of the cabin and knocked hard. No answer.

She pulled it open and stepped into the kitchen.

Dirty dishes were stacked in the sink and on the counter. Smitty used to complain that Gray was a neat freak.

"Gray?" she called out, fighting back waves of panic.

No. She wouldn't give him the power to hurt her, ever again.

He was sprawled out on a plaid couch in the living room, wearing his boxers.

She could smell the rum oozing out of his pores from across the room.

He was out cold.

She picked up the half full bottles of Captain Morgan's on the coffee table and poured them down the sink.

Smitty was getting even. He knew how much she hated housework.

She grabbed a garbage bag and tidied up then filled the sink with soapy water. It took two hours to finish the dishes and get the place in respectable shape, although she didn't venture into the bedroom.

She filled a glass she'd just washed with cold water, pulled Gray's boxer shorts, and poured the cold water over his balls.

"Shit," he yelled. He sat up and focused his eyes. "Amy?"

Before she could answer, he took hold of her waist and pulled her under him on the couch. He put his mouth on hers, and she turned her face away.

"Gray, get off me," she said.

He took hold of her chin. "Your eyes. They're different." He sounded angry and let her go.

She laughed, remembering the love-struck idiot she had been for him for so long. "Imagine that."

"Why are you here?

"Luke came to see me. Liz almost shot him. She has a concealed weapon permit, you know, and police connections."

"Luke needs to shut the fuck up."

"Well, you're conscious. I cleaned the filth, except for your bedroom. You look like shit. My work here is done."

"Is it now?" he said.

"I'm taking a quick walk to the lake, and I'm leaving."

She left him, rolled up her jeans as high as she could, then stepped into the lake. The water was cold and clear. She could see her toes.

He'd reached for her as if he cared.

She walked out of the water and to her car.

Her purse, phone, and keys were gone.

"Seriously?" she yelled.

Crime was nearly non-existent up here, wasn't it?

"Fuck," she yelled.

There was no help for it. She had to back inside.

❧❧❧

She was pissed, and Gray's dick was so hard it could cut glass. He'd slipped out to her car, military style, while she was in the lake and hid her stuff under his bed. He's even had time for a shower and shave, military fast. He'd brushed his teeth and pulled on a pair of jeans.

He had one more chance with her. He couldn't fuck it up. "What's wrong, angel face?"

She snorted. "Angel face?"

"Well, you cleaned up and shit."

"And shit." She set her mouth in a hard line he'd never seen before. He hated it. "My stuff, I left it in the car, and it's gone, all of it," she said.

"Tsk, tsk. You work at a resort. You know better."

"We're in the middle of nowhere," she screamed.

His cock twitched.

"Can I use your phone?"

"Nope," he said, trying hard to keep a straight face.

"Why?"

"My phone died, and I don't have a charger."

"You're fucking kidding me?"

"Nope," he shrugged.

"No landline?" she said.

"Nope," he said.

She narrowed her beautiful blue eyes. "If you say nope one more time, I'll hurt you."

He thought of her soft hands on his body, and his dick hardened to the point of pain.

She stomped into the kitchen and drank a glass of water.

She had to feel something for him if she came to see him. A flame of hope winnowed its way through the brick wall he'd built around his heart since he'd turned his back on her on their wedding day.

"I'm going," she said.

"You are?" He looked at her tank top that hugged her breasts, tight jeans that clung to her hips and ass, and flip flops.

She raised her eyebrows. "To civilization. Unless you know how to hotwire a car?"

"Nope."

She punched him hard in the gut. He grabbed her wrist and pulled her closer, breathing in her flowery scent. His other hand went to her waist, and his erection nudged her flat stomach.

"I'm not pregnant, by the way," she said with a catch to her voice.

He held her gently and nuzzled her ear. "I know," he said.

She stared up at him. "How?"

He took hold of her chin. "You'd have said, angel face."

She started to say something, then stopped and pulled away from him. "I'm going."

"Wait."

"No."

He had to change tactics fast. He pulled a can of bug repellent out of a closet and tossed it to her. She caught it easily.

"So you don't get too chewed up." He handed her half full bag of potato chips. "Toss this between you and the bears. They've been in the trash cans."

"Fine," she said, stomping out the front door.

"Amy, I'll take you, on the bike," he said. She'd have to hold onto him.

She set down the chips.

He went into his bedroom and pulled on a black T-shirt and leather boots. He grabbed a leather jacket, a pair of his mother's old tennis shoes, some socks, and a helmet.

Chapter 4

Amy's mouth went dry. How could she still want him?

He handed her his leather jacket and helmet.

"It's hot," she said. "And you're not wearing any-thing."

He waggled his eyebrows.

"I mean—"

"Put 'em on, Amy or I'm not taking you." He looked at her feet. "Sit."

She thumped down on the couch. He slipped her flip flops off and pulled the socks over her feet and up her calves.

She felt shivery.

Crap. His jacket smelled like him, and she would have to hold onto his six pack.

"Give me a minute." He went outside.

She decided the jacket and helmet were good things. They would put more distance between them. She detested him. How could he affect her still? By her calculations, the nearest town was about a half hour away. She could call Liz or her parents to come and get her. She kept a spare set of keys at her place. No way was Gray driving her back home.

She'd come here for Smitty. Gray was conscious. She was square.

∽∾∽∾

Gray grabbed a hose and gas can from the shed, stuck it in the tank, and sucked hard, draining most of the fuel out of the tank. He stowed the can and hose then ran to the lake, kicked off his boots, and stripped out of his jeans. He walked into the lake and rinsed the smell and taste of gasoline off his face and out of his mouth with lake water. He pulled his jeans back on, hoping she wouldn't notice his legs were damp.

"Gray?"

"Back here." He pulled his boots on and sprinted toward his bike. She walked hesitantly toward him. He'd never taken her on his bike before. "Have you ever ridden?"

He stared hard into her beautiful, troubled blue eyes, remembering how she rode him when she'd given him her virginity. It made him sick to know that he and Smitty had put the pain there, him with his deceit and Smitty with his lies.

And he was deceiving her now because he couldn't let her leave him. He held out his hand. She grasped it, and he pulled her closer.

"Smitty lied."

She looked surprised. He didn't press it.

"Straddle it," he said, shutting his eyes. He remembered how she looked when she'd straddled him and the love in her eyes as she looked down at him.

Was there any left? Could he nurse it to life again?

She sat on the bike and tugged at her helmet. "I hate this. You're not wearing one."

Her incredible eyes flashed midnight blue, and he quashed the urge to fuse his mouth to hers.

"I only have one," he said.

"Then I'm not wearing one either." She tugged on the strap.

He took hold of her waist then palmed her breasts. They were as perfect as he remembered. He tweaked her nipples then let her go. She was breathing hard.

Thank fuck. He still affected her.

"Yes, you are." He got on the bike. "Hold onto my waist and lean into the turns like I do."

Her soft little hands clutched the sides of his waist. He shuddered.

"No," he said. He took hold of her hands and wrapped them around his waist. His erection nearly burst through his pants. "Like this."

He started the engine.

Thank fuck this was going to be a short ride.

☙❧

Gray's bike sputtered. Amy gripped him tighter as he stopped. They'd been riding for about five minutes.

"I don't trust it, Angel Face, we're going back."

He started it before she could say anything. They made it to the road the cabin was on when it sputtered again. Gray restarted it, and they coasted to the end of the drive leading up to the cabin on fumes. He helped Amy off the bike then pushed it to the cottage.

"Wait," she said. "I've still got daylight. I'm going to walk."

She took off the helmet and shrugged out of the jacket, taking one last whiff before she handed it to him.

She missed his sharp intake of breath as he watched her sniff the leather.

Gray popped the kickstand and took hold of her hand.

"You'll be bear bait, Angel. They feed this time of day. Let me feed you. We'll sleep on it and figure something out in the morning."

∽✺∽

His eyes blazed gold. He brought her hand to his lips and kissed it. "Please."

His lips on her palm zinged through her nerves, and her muscles tightened in her core.

How could he affect her this way? *Think of his face when he left you standing in front of your family and friends in your wedding dress.* She pulled her hand away. "All right. I can do the couch for one night," she said. "You seemed to be comfortable."

"You get the bed, Angel." He opened the door and put his hand on the small of her back to guide her inside. She flinched away from his touch.

His bed would smell like him.

"No way. If the bedroom is anything like the rest of this place was, no thanks."

"I'll clean it up," he said.

They sat on Adirondack chairs outside near the grill. You could see the lake. Gray had started a fire in the pit. He'd unearthed turkey burgers and buns from the freezer and opened a can of three-bean salad. He also found a bottle of pinot grigio his mother must have purchased from a winery in Grand Traverse.

Amy was on her fourth glass. Gray drank diet Coke. The sun hadn't set yet.

"You good, Angel?"

He had to stop calling her that.

"No."

Crap. Had she said that out loud?

He laughed. "Yes."

Wood smoke wafted through the air, and she watched the waves gently lap the rocky shore. A steady breeze kept the flies and mosquitos at bay.

Yeah, she was good.

He chuckled.

She clamped her hand over her mouth. She had to stop doing that. She stared into the flames. He dropped another log on the fire. She took a sip of the crisp, dry wine, remembered her last bonfire, and chuckled bitterly.

"What?"

The chairs were close enough together that he could touch her, but he didn't.

"My last fire, I burned everything from you and me

at Liz' parent's place in Petoskey."

He reached for her left hand then lifted it. She still had an indentation from wearing his engagement ring.

"I still have it, haven't gotten to the pawn shop. Is it real, by the way? Or as fake as everything else was? It will save me a trip, unless you want it back. Actually, tough shit if you do."

"Smitty lied. He said you two did things."

"He was jealous of you," Amy blurted out, feeling disloyal to Smitty.

She yanked her hand out of Gray's grasp. She had slurred her words a bit and set down her wine glass.

"We had a code." He stared into the flames. "He knew how much I wanted you, but he got to you first at that damn frat party. So he technically saw you first. That was that."

"So you wanted to add me to the list of your fuck buddies," Amy snorted then winced. She sounded disgusting when she snorted.

"No, Angel, you don't."

Crap. She'd done it again.

"I love that," he said. "I always know what you're thinking."

He put another log on the fire and kept his back to her. "I saw your face, Amy, when I was with who you call my fuck buddies. And called your name more than once, which they didn't appreciate. They didn't mean anything. That makes me a douche, but it's true. When Smitty died, I went crazy. They offer you help, but nobody takes it. The code, you know. Man up, never complain, never explain."

"I miss him, and I couldn't go to his funeral." Amy let her tears fall. "You think I don't know it was my fault?"

"No, Amy."

"There was never a good time. I thought I should have ended it before you left, but it seemed cruel."

"He didn't love you the way you deserve or want you like I did, like I do," he said.

The sun had set. She couldn't see his expression in the shadows.

"You can't," she said. "I don't believe you. I can't believe you ever again."

"One more night," he said. "I just want to hold you, that's all."

He held out his hand. She took it. He pulled her up, and she swayed. He swung her up into his arms and carried her to the bedroom.

He helped her to step out of her jeans then slipped her tank top over her head. He took off his T-shirt, unhooked her bra, and slipped his shirt over her head.

Why was she letting him do this? Because she was woozy from wine?

He chuckled.

She'd spoken out loud again. Damn.

She put her arms through Gray's shirt and sighed. It smelled like him.

"Is that a good thing?

She didn't bother trying to lie. "God, yes. Did you put truth serum in the wine?"

"In vino, veritas," he murmured.

He took off his jeans and slid in beside her in bed, pulling his back to her chest. She could feel his erection through his boxers.

"That's so not happening," she said, edging away from him.

He pulled her back against him. "I just want to hold you," he said against her ear. "I'll survive. It's been my normal state for a while now. Difference is, you're here in the flesh and not just in my head."

She felt so tired. She shut her eyes and relaxed against him.

ↁↂↁ

"Amy."

She opened her eyes. In her sleep, she must have

turned toward Gray. Her cheek rested on his chest. He was drenched in sweat, shaking and asleep.

"Amy," he moaned.

"Gray." She shook him. 'Wake up."

He opened his eyes and looked confused. He took hold of her waist. "Amy?"

"You were having a dream."

"You're real. And safe. Thank fuck."

His mouth crashed down on hers. His tongue sought entry. She opened willingly and was lost. His tongue plunged and retreated, mimicking his cock plunging into her sheath. His erection nudged her slit, which was wet. His hands left her waist and caressed her breasts while he continued to plunder her mouth.

He let her go and rose above her.

"Say you want this."

She moaned and rubbed against him.

His eyes blazed gold. He caressed her swollen lips with the pad of his thumb and waited. "The words, Angel, say the words."

"Please, Gray. I want you, I want this."

Chapter 5

Gray tried to go slow, but her little moans undid him. He plunged into her slick channel, hitting her sweet spot. Amy spasmed around him and screamed his name. He pressed his thumb on her clit.

"Come again for me, Angel."

She did, and he emptied himself inside her. He turned them so he was still inside her and she drifted back to sleep.

He couldn't let her go. He didn't deserve her, but he knew his life would be nothing without her—his sweet angel.

He'd had the dream again. He, Luke, and Smitty had

seen unspeakable things in Afghanistan, brutality inflicted on women and children. This time in his dream, the victim was Amy.

When he opened his eyes, and she was in his arms, his world switched back to color, the world he'd glimpsed when she gifted him with her virginity, a world he thought he didn't deserve when Smitty died.

She murmured his name against his chest. He held her tighter in his arms. Would she ever forgive him? And if she did, could he live with the fact that everyone who cared about her would likely hate him for the rest of his life?

She snuggled into his chest and sighed.

Fuck, yes.

He could endure anything for this.

She was his, and he was hers as long as she drew breath. He had to man up and make it happen. He'd faced fire from insurgents, he could do this.

He didn't close his eyes until the sun inched over the horizon.

ოჳოჳ

Amy dreamed she was in Gray's arms. She pressed her cheek into her pillow. It was warm and rock hard. Her eyes flew open.

It was real.

He was real.

Holy hell, he was still inside her.

She really had to pee.

She pulled away from him. He mumbled when she edged away from him but didn't open his eyes.

She had to process this. She tip-toed into the bathroom and shut the door. His cum was sticky on her thighs.

Holy hell.

He came inside her.

She took deep breaths and tried to think. She was due for her period in a couple of days, so she shouldn't be pregnant. Why did she feel disappointed?

He'd asked her. He'd made her say she wanted him. Had he said he loved her last night, by the fire?

She ran water in the sink as quietly as she could and cleaned herself up.

Her clothes, she needed her clothes.

He undressed her. Did he leave them on the floor?

She walked as softly as she could into the bedroom and saw her stuff in a pile on the floor. She crawled on all fours to get it and glanced under the bed.

Her purse—he'd taken her purse and hidden it there.

She took it, grabbed her clothes, scrambled into the living room, and got dressed. She opened her purse—her keys, phone, and wallet were there. She opened the front door, slipped outside, and got behind her steering wheel, blinking back tears.

Why was she hesitating?

She'd done what she came to do. How could she even think of being with someone who had hurt her with such cruelty?

Liz and her parents would likely stage an intervention.

He left her at the altar with malice and forethought.

How could she trust him not to abandon her again or that he wasn't playing games?

How would she face her family and friends if she gave him another chance?

She thought of all their faces on her so-called wedding day, then his face when he opened his eyes in the cabin when she shook him awake.

If she stayed, she was weak and pathetic.

Sobbing, she put the key in the ignition and drove into town.

❧❦❧

Gray rubbed his eyes and sat up. "Amy?"

A sense of dread settled in his chest. He looked under the bed.

Her purse was gone. He walked around the cabin, knowing without looking that her car was gone. He didn't blame her.

He walked to the beach, plunged into the cold water, and swam laps until he was exhausted.

His business.

He owed it to Luke to get back to work if they hadn't already gone bankrupt. He floated on his back and stared at the cloudless sky. It was the same color as Amy's eyes.

"Aren't you cold?"

It sounded like Amy.

Great, now he was hearing things.

Bam.

A Frisbee hit him in the head.

Amy.

He remembered from college she had great aim. He stood up in the water. He knew he was grinning like a fool.

She clutched a bag. His eyes raked over her tank top and jeans that hugged her curves. She'd pulled her hair up in a half-hearted pony-tail. He grabbed the Frisbee.

"I got donuts and coffee in town."

"You came back."

He wailed the Frisbee straight at her. She caught it easily, still holding the donuts.

He eyed the Frisbee. "Where'd you get that?"

"The hardware store."

She wailed it at his face. He caught it and threw it back just as hard. She threw it back even harder. He kept hold of it.

His grin nearly split his face in two. He stalked toward her. "You came back."

She stood her ground. "Obviously."

He took the bag of donuts out of her hand and set it on the ground. "Why?" He took hold of her face. "Tell me."

"My parents will kill me, and Liz will kill you," she said. "But this is nothing serious, Gray."

She loved him, he knew it, or she wouldn't have come back.

But she was scared.

And rightly so.

"No reason we can't be fuck buddies." She didn't look in his eyes when she said it.

So she wanted to lead him around by his balls. He'd let her. For a while.

"I bought some supplies, too." She pointed to a box of condoms on the Adirondack chair, ribbed, extra-large.

Game on.

Who was he to deny a lady?

He grabbed her by her waist and hoisted her over his shoulder.

"Wait," she squealed. "The donuts."

He stooped, still holding her, to pick up the condoms and the donuts and took her inside.

✷✷✷

Two weeks later:

He spent every night with her since they got back from the UP, usually at her apartment, although he had to drive an hour and a half one way to his office in Traverse City. They stayed at his condo in Traverse City on the weekend. He'd been gone a while Saturday morning and, when he came back, he had blood on his shirt.

"Holy hell, Gray," Amy squealed.

"I didn't see that. Bloody nose," he said.

He whipped his T-shirt off, and Amy sucked in her breath. Would she ever get used to his six-pack?

Would she want any other guy the way she wanted him when this was over?

His eyes blazed gold. "Come here, Amy."

She hadn't said those words out loud, did she?

"What words, Angel?"

He pulled her against him and lowered his mouth to hers. His kiss was gentle. He traced the outline of her lips with his tongue then sucked gently on her bottom lip before he drew away and rested his forehead on hers.

Amy's breathing came in ragged gasps.

"Can you take some time off, week after next?" he said.

His eyes blazed gold again. "Yes," she said. "Why?"

"It's a surprise," he said.

"I don't like your surprises," she said.

The gold lights died in his eyes. Amy bit back an apology.

"I'll never hurt you again, Amy, I promise. On Smitty's grave."

Holy hell.

He set his mouth in a tight line. She longed to soften it. Her fingers traced the contours of his beautiful lips.

"Okay," she said. She trailed her fingers through the smattering of hair on his chest, then over his tight, flat nipples. He growled. "You have to tell me what to pack,' she said.

He took hold of the T-shirt she wore and pulled it over her head then made short work of her bra.

"As little as possible," he said. He lowered his mouth to her nipple and laved it with his tongue, then did the same to its twin.

She moaned. Her knees felt like jelly. He lifted her in his arms and strode to his bedroom.

Keep it light, nothing serious.

∽∾∽

He didn't tell her she said the words out loud or tell her how deadly serious he was, serious enough to let her father punch him in the face when he asked him and Amy's mother to fly to Las Vegas so he and Amy could get married for real—if she would have him.

There was a good chance she wouldn't.

And he would give her the chance to reject him publicly in front of her family and friends, if that was what she wanted.

He lowered her onto the bed.

Did she know she murmured her love for him, called his name, and reached for his dick in her sleep?

She wouldn't utter those words he so longed to hear when she was awake.

But he could make her say she wanted him, and she screamed his name when he made her come.

And she did before she dozed in his arms after he gently cleaned her up and disposed of his condom. Her vanilla scent wafted over him. He stroked her silky hair.

He could fix this.

He had to fix this.

He had heaven in his grasp in the meadow on the day she believed was her wedding day.

He'd spend the rest of his life adoring her if she let him.

Chapter 6

Gray drove them to the small airport in Traverse City. Luke had his pilot's license, and he was flying them to the destination that Gray refused to divulge. He even enlisted Liz, who was barely civil to him, to pack her bag, and swore her to secrecy, to Amy's amazement.

Liz sat in the front of the plane, snarling at Luke.

Amy and Gray sat in the back. He kept his hand possessively on her thigh. Liz saw it and glared at him. He ignored her. He didn't take his eyes off Amy.

"Are you okay with small planes?"

She shrugged. "A plane is a plane. I'm okay with smooth flights."

He smiled at her and traced circles on her bare leg. The clingy wrap dress had seemed like a good idea, but now she wasn't so sure.

The plane taxied down the runway. She put her head on Gray's shoulder. He shuddered. She moved away from him, but he gently drew her back.

"No, Angel, I like it." He lowered his voice. "I love it."

His eyes blazed gold. Liz glared at her.

Amy shut her eyes. She'd popped a Valium earlier. She settled into the crook of his neck. He smelled like cologne and that smell that was only him.

She wanted this.

She wanted him.

It didn't make her weak if this was her choice, did it?

He murmured soothing words against her ear she couldn't make out over the roar of the engine as Luke took flight.

West, they were flying west.

She let sleep take her as he stroked her hair.

When she opened her eyes, her mouth was so dry she could barely swallow.

"Here." He gave her a twenty-four-ounce bottle of water. "Drink as much of this as you can. I should have woken you."

"Vegas, Amy, we're landing in Sin City," Liz said.

"And we're going to be bad." She looked daggers at Gray.

Luke began the descent. Amy had slept for over three hours.

At her mother's urging, she had gotten some Valium from her doctor after her wedding fiasco to soothe her nerves. It knocked her on her butt. She made a note to flush the rest and guzzled the water.

He looked concerned. "Are you okay?"

She smiled. "Note to self. No more Valium."

Liz swiveled in her seat. "Her doctor gave it to her after you fucked up the wedding. She couldn't stop crying."

"Liz—" Amy said.

He frowned as the wheels touched down and lugged both their suitcases down the steps.

"Hi, baby."

Amy gasped.

Her parents stood next to an Escalade. Gray set down the cases and squeezed her hand. Liz continued to frown at Gray, Amy's father Steve snarled at Luke and her mother Nancy smiled nervously.

"What's happening?" she said.

The hot, dry desert air seemed to swallow her up.

Gray kissed her, hard, possessively, and stepped away. "See you tomorrow, Angel."

He and Luke got into a Range Rover and sped away.

Nancy guided Amy into the back seat of the SUV. "Sit down, baby, you've gone pale."

Liz sat in the front with her dad, who still scowled.

"This was Gray's brilliant idea, a Vegas wedding," Liz said.

Her voice dripped acid, and Steve let loose with a stream of expletives that had Liz turning around in her seat. Her mouth gaped open.

"Steve, stop it," Nancy said.

Her father had never used a curse word in front of her or her brother Kyle before.

"Is Kyle here?" Amy said.

"His flight comes in late. Gray was determined. He wants everything to be as close to before…" Her mother's voice trailed off. "He didn't even flinch when your father punched him in the face."

"His bloody nose," Amy said.

"He even had me help him reorder your same wedding dress after yours was—" Nancy said.

Liz swiveled in her seat. "Burned, we burned it up. And this can be exactly the same as before Ames. You dump his ass in front of everyone, this time. And tonight we have a wild girl night. In fact, we should bring the guys we hook up with to the wedding."

Nancy winced, and Steve let loose with another stream of expletives.

Amy had never seen her dad so agitated. "Dad, are you okay?"

"Listen, doll, I'll walk you down the aisle or whatever it is, if that's what you want. But I can't promise I won't beat his face in when we get up there. Just saying." He shrugged.

"Darling, he's a combat-trained Marine," Nancy said. "He could kill you if he wanted. He just takes whatever you dish out."

They pulled onto the strip then into the MGM Grand.

"He's paying for all this," Nancy said. "Our flights and rooms."

"Mom, do you want me to marry him?" Amy said out of earshot of Liz and her dad.

"I want what you want, always," Nancy said. "Be clear in your mind. But I do know this. That man isn't leaving your life without a fight. And he knows how to fight."

"Is Gray staying here, too?" Amy said.

"I don't know," Nancy said.

They walked through the marble lobby and golden lion. The slot machines dinged in the background.

"Over the Rainbow," Liz said.

"Things are set for tomorrow morning," Nancy said. "Eleven o'clock."

They checked in. Amy and Liz were on the same floor as Nancy and Steve, but at opposite ends of the long hallway.

"Your wedding stuff is with us," Steve said. "If you do decide to do this, you should probably be here at ten."

"I'm taking him to dinner then letting him loose at the blackjack table," Nancy said.

Her father grunted as he slid the key into the slot. He turned abruptly and pulled Amy in for a big bear hug. Amy choked back tears.

He kissed the top of her head. "Be sure, baby, whatever you decide. Leave his ass up there, stand him up, or—" He gritted his teeth. "—marry him. We support you." He kissed her cheek and let her go.

Liz let them into their room. There were two queen size beds and a view of the Vegas skyline. The room was decorated in plum and rich brown with cream accents.

"Executive queen suite," Liz said. "Too bad we're not spending any time here, though."

She opened her suitcase and pulled out a short, clingy red dress that dipped low in the front and spiky, fuck-me-red heels.

"Go, Liz," Amy said.

"Oh, no, Ames, this is for you. Not negotiable. It's Sin City. Everyone wears this."

Amy wiggled into it. She stared at her reflection. The dress hugged her curves and showed cleavage. The heels made her legs look longer than her respectable five foot seven. Amy couldn't bring herself to take it off.

"Makeup and hair, next. Sit."

Amy let Liz go wild. Amy gasped when Liz had finished. Liz had coaxed Amy's blonde hair into soft waves and went dramatic with brown-black eyeliner and red lipstick that matched the dress.

"Wow," Liz said. Liz looked demure by comparison in a short, flirty, black skirt and sleeveless polka dot blouse and pink lipstick.

"Liz, this is too much. I look like I'm looking to hook up."

"You are," Liz said.

"I'm not," Amy said. "No matter what I do tomorrow, I'm not doing that tonight." She kicked off the spiky heels.

"No, Ames. This is Vegas. You'll totally blend and, whatever you do or don't do tonight, whatever happens in Vegas stays in Vegas."

Liz fished a little clutch purse out of Amy's suitcase. Amy put some cash, her ID, room key, and lipstick into the purse as Liz sang "Luck Be A Lady Tonight" and opened the door.

⋐⋑⋐⋑

Amy's heels click-clacked on the lobby floor of the hotel. Every male head swiveled.

Gray's guts churned, and he was instantly hard. She hadn't seen him, and he stepped behind a pillar. Her dress covered her sweet ass barely and hugged her curves. Her legs went on forever, and her neckline showed the cleft in her luscious breasts. He was so hard it was painful. Liz was talking to one of the valets while Amy shifted in those damned fuck-me heels.

"Let's go," Luke said. He could tell the second Luke saw Amy. He stopped short.

"Don't. Fucking. Look. At. Her. Go get the car," Gray said.

"Good luck with that," Luke muttered.

The valet handed Liz and Amy into a cab and took a good, long look at Amy's ass when she got in. Gray squelched the urge to put his fist in the guy's face and pulled out a fifty dollar bill.

He twisted his face into a smile and walked up to the valet, letting him see the bill he held in his hand.

"Where are they headed? She's mine, the blonde. We're getting married tomorrow."

The valet frowned.

Gray saw a tattoo on the guy's wrist: *2nd Cav.* "Afghanistan?"

The valet nodded. "You?" he asked.

"Marine reserves."

The valet waved the fifty away and named a club that Gray had never heard of. "It's new. You got GPS?"

Gray nodded. "The brunette wanted the name of a club where—just get there fast, man."

Luke pulled up the Mustang they'd rented.

Traffic on the strip crawled, but Gray figured Amy and Liz's cab was stuck in the same traffic. Unless the cabbie knew a back way to the club, which was likely.

"Fuck."

"We're five minutes behind them," Luke said.

"What if someone messes with her drink? Fuck," Gray yelled.

Luke recalibrated the GPS, made a series of turns off the strip, and ended up at the back door of the club. He parked the Mustang next to the building. They walked in the back entrance through a hallway with closed doors on each side, bypassing the bouncer.

"Give me the keys."

Luke did, and Gray dropped them into his pocket.

He scanned the packed dance floor. Amy was sandwiched between two guys. One of the fuckers had his hand on her hips. Gray couldn't see her face. Liz saw them and grinned. She chanted "blow job, blow job."

The guy with his hands on Amy lifted her over his head. She was passed up to the bar, spread out on top of it, and given a shot of something white she was supposed to swallow all at once. She did it, to the applause of the crowd.

Gray pushed his way toward her, took hold of her waist, and pulled her off the bar and into his arms. She struggled.

"It's me, Angel," he said. She sagged against him, and he fused his mouth to hers. She sighed. Liz stood next to Amy. "Give her air and get out. This is her night."

He kept her anchored to him and tilted her chin up, tracing her lips with his thumb. "What do you want, Amy? You could spend it with me."

"Like hell," Liz sputtered.

Amy looked at Liz and pulled away from him. The moment she was free, some fucker grabbed hold of her and took her back on the dance floor. He was grinding his crotch against her ass. A red haze settled over Gray. Luke said something, but the words didn't penetrate through the haze.

The fucker had his hands on Amy's waist. When he

moved them up to her breasts, Gray didn't hear anything over the roaring in his ears.

Amy struggled to get free of the fucker. Gray moved fast and connected his fist with the asshole's jaw. The bouncer hadn't noticed yet. Gray took hold of her, carried her out the back door, put her in the car, and sped away toward the desert.

He struggled to keep his breathing even. She stared straight ahead.

"Sorry, Angel. Crowds get me sometimes. Then that fucker put his hands on you. I'll take you back if you want."

But he wouldn't let her out of his sight.

She didn't answer.

"Or we could look at the stars. It's a clear night."

Or she could tell him to fuck off.

"You never asked," she said.

"Asked what? You struggled when that guy touched you. I lost it."

"No—to marry you. You didn't ask."

"Amy—"

"Not now. Not after I said it."

He didn't ask because he was scared shitless she would turn him down.

The first time he asked her, she'd laughed and cried then said yes.

But it didn't count.

"The desert," she said. "I always wanted to see it at night." She pulled her phone out of her purse and texted. "Liz says she's going to kill you when we get back to Michigan and her dad and brother will cover it up. She carries a gun, a small one, a 22, and she knows how to shoot."

He laughed. "She's a good friend to you. My luck, my wife's best friend and parents will hate me till I die, maybe by Liz's trigger finger."

It would be worth it.

Chapter 7

Wife, he said wife like this was a done deal.

"And all your Marine buddies will always think of me as the bitch who dumped Smitty and sent him to his death. You have to see we can't—"

Gray covered her mouth with his hand. "Let's look at the stars. We—me, Luke, and Smitty—did that on cold winter nights when we were deployed."

He lifted his hand, and she got out of the car. He left the headlights on and was instantly at her side.

"Stay close," he said. "Snakes." "Smitty hated snakes."

"And peanut butter," Amy said.

"And every care package we got had stuff with peanut butter," he said. "He was so pissed."

"Not the ones I sent."

"I know. I was jealous as hell. And he liked that. He'd rub it in my face."

Gray took her hand and walked her to the front of the Mustang. He lifted her so she sat on the hood.

She stared at the scrub on the ground around them, disappointed there was no cactus.

"We can find some cactus if you want."

She'd spoken out loud again. "You know you're the only person I do that to."

The night air was cool, and she shivered. He settled them both on the hood of the car and put his arm around her.

"Lean back," he said.

She did. Her legs dangled toward the ground. Her dress rode up around her waist, exposing her thong. She tried to tug the dress down to no avail.

"No one can see," he said against her ear. His hand moved to cup her smooth mound. He made a low rumble in his throat. "This is new," he said.

She was glad it was dark. She lifted her palm to her heated face. "I did it when we got here."

"Sin City. For girl's night or for me?" His voice was strained.

He slipped his thumb under her thong.

"That's the question, isn't it?" she said.

"Mmmm."

His thumb moved to her clit, and his other hand found her nipple. Her body danced to life. He slipped a thick finger inside her.

She was wet.

He pulled her dress down in front, then her half-bra, and sucked on her nipple. He rubbed her clit then found her g-spot, and she went off like a rocket, screaming his name.

When she came back to herself, he stood on the ground and had hold of her waist.

His cock teased the juncture of her thighs, and her thong was gone.

"Indulge me, Angel. Since we picked this car up, all I could think of was having you on the hood."

He thrust into her, hitting the back of her womb. She moaned.

He stopped. "Did I hurt you?"

"God, no."

A condom, he wasn't wearing a condom.

"Gray?"

He thrust again, dragging his cock against her sensitive bundle of nerves. She moaned.

"Wait for me, Angel. I want us to go together."

He thrust harder and faster. She gripped his waist, digging her nails into his skin.

"Condom," she said.

"I can't stop." He pressed his thumb over her clit. "Now."

She exploded into a thousand points of light like the starry desert night as he groaned her name and emptied his seed inside her. He dropped his weight on top of her, and she put her arms around him and stroked his dark, wavy hair, damp with sweat. She was always amazed how soft it felt.

"I love you, Amy. I would stay inside you forever, if I could. You're full of my cum," he murmured. He made no effort to move.

God help her, she wanted his babies. She'd cried buckets when she discovered she wasn't pregnant after their first time.

She was a stupid fool. He betrayed her.

She was crazy to trust him.

What was wrong with her?

He sighed and pulled out of her slowly.

"Nothing, Angel. There's nothing wrong with you."

Crap. How much had she said out loud?"

"You are crazy to trust me. Stay there."

She couldn't move if she had to. He opened the car door then strode back to her, naked from the waist down.

He was magnificent.

"You, my darling fiancée, are a vision from heaven."

He held a small tissue box and cleaned her then put the box in her hands.

"For later," He traced her mouth with the pad of his thumb. "I'm crazy, too. Crazy in love with you. Always have been. Should have broken the guy code and been honest with you in college. And with Smitty. Is it wrong to hate him?"

She made a move to sit up, but he stopped her.

"The sight and thought of you filled with my cum…" He shut his eyes. "Please, stay still for just a while longer."

Amy shivered, but not from the cold. He shook out his pants, pulled them on and reached in his pocket. He pulled out a box, opened it, took out a ring, and slipped it on her nerveless finger. He stroked her hair.

"Wear this for me, just for tonight if that's all there is. Under the starlight and moonlight."

She held her hand up. The stone looked like an emerald-cut, but she couldn't tell for sure in the dark. He lifted her into his arms and settled them in the backseat of the Mustang, cradling her in his lap so she could see the stars through the open sunroof.

His heart thudded against her ear, and she shut her eyes.

She didn't know she told him she loved him while she slept.

Chapter 8

Fuck," Liz was trying to make coffee. She had dark circles under her eyes and looked deathly pale.

"Going for I-Zombie?" Amy said. She brushed her friend aside. "You have to plug it in."

"You ditched me," Liz said. "I'm not talking to you."

"Yes, you are. You're my maid of honor, and you love me."

Liz grunted.

"It looks like you had fun," Amy continued. "You got back after I did. What did you do?"

Liz grunted again and gulped down the coffee Amy

gave her. Amy had made it double strength. She winced when she drank it. But she finished it anyway. She power-showered and wrapped her hair in a towel. Liz went next.

Amy ordered bagels from room service, and they came by the time Liz emerged from the bathroom. Liz eyed the tray first then took a bite.

"There's cream cheese."

Liz shuddered.

"I'll take that as a no."

"What are you going to do, Amy?"

Amy stared at the ring glittering on her finger and blinked back tears. "Last night was amazing."

Liz let loose with a stream of impressive expletives.

Amy could be pregnant. She did the math. She was early enough in her cycle. "I don't know, Liz. He knows you and Dad will hate him forever." She hugged her friend. "And he knows neither of you is going anywhere."

Liz pulled away. "Think of the look on his face when he rejected you, Amy. He's a cold-hearted dick."

Amy did remember, especially the way he looked when he walked away from her. Her chest tightened.

She could do the same thing. He was giving her the chance to do the same thing.

She loved him beyond reason, but could she trust him?

Liz touched her shoulder and sighed. "Let's do this."

Amy squared her shoulders. "Or not," she said.

$$\backsim\!\backsim$$

The chapel was somewhat tasteful and filled with hydrangeas. Amy's brother Kyle hugged her hard in their parent's hotel room and offered to kick Gray's ass.

Gray's parents sat in the front of the chapel, smiling nervously. Amy walked down the aisle on her father's arm as Gray stood soldier straight next to Luke, who looked worse than Liz did.

What was up with that?

Amy wore the same style wedding dress she did before that he had procured with help from her mother. His eyes blazed gold when she stood next to him. Her father kissed her cheek and snarled at Gray before he took his seat with her mother.

The minister started speaking, but Amy couldn't process the words. Gray didn't take his eyes off her. Liz shook her head and glared at him. The minister got to the part asking if anyone objected.

Liz erupted. "He doesn't love her."

Luke screamed in reply. "Yes, he does. He knows

she can leave him up here. He's giving her the chance to get even if she wants."

The minister paused, likely used to crazy Vegas weddings, and raised his eyebrows in silent question.

Amy stayed quiet. The minister continued. Some of the words penetrated through her hazy brain. They hadn't made it this far before.

Would she take him as her husband?

Would she love him, comfort him, honor him in sickness and in health, forsaking all others; be faithful till death?

Death.

Smitty was gone.

And they were alive—damaged, but alive.

Everyone waited.

Gray's eyes looked wild. "Marry me," he mouthed. "I love you, so much," he whispered, reached for her hand, brought her palm to his lips, and waited.

"All right," Amy said so low the minister had to lean forward to hear her.

Gray motioned with his other hand for the man to continue. The minister shrugged and repeated the words to him.

"I take you, Amy, as my wedded wife, to have and to hold." His eyes lost their wild look though they still blazed gold. "This is my solemn vow."

The minister touched her arm. "You sure about this, honey?"

She looked at Gray.

This was her chance. She'd given him hope. She could rip it away like a bandage covering a fresh wound. Tears streamed down her mother's face. She mouthed "Love you."

Her brother clenched and unclenched his fists, and her father frowned. Liz said her name in a low voice.

His solemn vow.

Amy somehow knew that he had made a vow to avenge Smitty's death and followed it through, although it nearly destroyed her—and him. Nearly.

But they were alive, or she was now.

She'd been half-dead for weeks after he walked away from her and, apparently, so had he until she showed up at the cabin.

The emerald-cut diamond caught the light and glittered on her finger. He still held her hand. She pulled it free. He took a step back away from her. His eyes were glassy and unfocused.

"Yes," Liz said.

Amy shook her head and moved toward him. She caressed his hard, handsome face she loved so much. "Smitty was a dick," she said.

The minister gasped.

Gray's eyes blazed gold. "He goddamn lied," he said.

"You believed him."

"I believe in you, and in us," he said.

She looked at the minister and nodded. "I'm sure, sir."

Gray didn't wait for the final pronouncement but claimed her mouth, as if she was more important to him than his next breath. Amy sucked on his tongue, and he lifted his mouth from hers, adjusting his trousers.

"You'll pay for that Angel."

She smiled into his eyes. "I hope so."

He threw back his head and laughed then swooped her into his arms and spun them around. "I love you, wedded wife, so much."

"I love you, wedded husband."

The small crowd, except for Liz, erupted in applause as he carried her down the aisle.

"Would have lost a bet on that one," the minister said, shaking his head.

"Is there a reception?" Amy said. "I never asked."

"A very short one for us," he said.

And it was.

Epilogue

Fifteen months later:

Amy flipped through her text messages. "Mom and Dad are coming over."

Gray kissed the spot at the nape of her neck that drove her wild. "The babies are sleeping. It's a bad time," he said. "Text them back."

"They're half-way here." She sighed. "I can't."

"That means we have time. Text them back and ask them to stop and buy something that will give us more time."

His hands moved to her breasts. She'd tried to

breastfeed, but Jack and Jordan were a hungry handful, and she only did it for the first three months.

She picked up her cell.

"Send them to Sam's Club for diapers. It will be packed," he said.

His hand moved under the waistband of the yoga pants she lived in. His and Luke's building business was doing so well that they both agreed she would stay home with the babies, for now, anyway. It had been six months, and she hadn't missed her marketing job too much so far.

She sent the text.

Her mom texted back "no prob."

"We have lots of diapers," she said.

"They don't know that," he said.

He moved them upstairs to their bedroom. Jack and Jordan slept in the second bedroom of their cramped con-do.

"We have to look for a house," she said.

"Mmmm."

Luke and Gray's company had so many orders, they were expanding, and she and Gray could easily afford to move someplace bigger. He dispensed with her bra and pressed her down on their bed. He sucked hard on first one, then the other, nipple. "I got a taste," he said.

His words comforted her. She missed nursing. He yanked her pants off and moved his mouth lower, kissing her faint stretch marks he'd rubbed coconut butter on each night when she was pregnant. The twins came fast and easily, and she hadn't needed a C-section.

Gray sucked on her bundle of nerves, and she came hard, moaning his name. He inserted one finger inside her, then, two, massaging her sweet spot till she shuddered her release again. His cock pressed the juncture of her thighs, and he entered her slowly.

His eyes never left her face. "Are you sore, baby? You're so tight."

"No silly. It's been six months."

He'd been so careful with her after the twins came, too careful, something she intended to change right then.

She met his thrust, clenching her inner muscles around him. "Please, Gray."

He eased out of her and teased her nipples to hard peaks.

"Faster, harder, I won't break."

He kissed her harder, and she sucked on his tongue, which she knew made him crazy. "I don't want to hurt you," he said when he tore his mouth away from her lips. "You are more precious to me than my life."

"You couldn't, you won't." She knew that in her bones. She also knew it almost killed him to walk away from her in the meadow that day.

He stilled. "Don't, Angel. Don't go back there, ever, please."

She gasped as he plunged and hit her sweet spot. "How do you know?" she said.

He always knew when she thought of that day.

His eyes blazed gold. "The light goes out of your beautiful eyes. I was fucked up, crazy in love with you, but fucked up."

He surged again, hitting the back of her womb. She moaned and remembered his face when she said she would marry him, when she could have left him standing there in front of the minister, in front of their families and friends as he did to her, but she couldn't. She was crazy in love with him, too.

"Get out of my head," she said, trying to glare at him.

He thrust against her clit that time, and she dug her nails into his shoulders. He loved it when she left marks on him.

"Never, I love being inside you, Angel. You fill me with light."

His voice faltered, and she kissed him hard. She moved her hands to his flanks and tore his mouth away.

"Ladies choice?" she said.

"What do you have in mind, wedded wife?"

"Me on top, wedded husband."

He chuckled and rolled them over, managing to stay inside her.

"How did you do that?" she said.

"Inside you, Angel, always inside you." He put his hands behind his head. "Have at it."

She lifted herself off him and bent down to lick his flat nipples then his six pack, making her way slowly to his cock. He groaned. She sucked the tip, tasting pre cum, and took him as deep as she could. He urged her up, and she moved reluctantly.

"I want to be inside you when I come," he said.

"So bossy," she said as she impaled him inside her.

"You love it."

She did.

He bucked, and she moaned.

"Look at me," he said. I want to see your sweet face when you ride me."

She stared into his brown eyes blazing gold that she loved so much, straightened up, and lowered herself up and down until he took control, as she knew and hoped he would.

"You feel like silk," he said just before he pressed his thumb onto her clit.

She came apart, screaming his name as he emptied himself inside her. She'd gone on injection birth control when she stopped nursing. She collapsed on top of him. He held her close.

"God, I love you," he said.

"I love you too, so much," she said, raising her head to stare at his face. She made a move to ease him out of her.

"No," he said. "Not yet."

She settled back against him with a sigh.

℃℃℃

Steve and Nancy pulled into the driveway of Gray and Amy's condo.

"Good thing I stopped for diapers this week," Nancy said.

"Yeah," Steve said. "Did you see what a madhouse that parking lot was?"

Nancy grabbed the boxes out of the trunk and handed them to Steve.

"Just go in," he said. "They know we're coming."

The door was unlocked, and Steve stopped short when he heard Amy scream Gray's name.

"Son of a bitch." He set down the diapers "Not again."

"Out, now," Nancy said.

They stepped outside and got back in their car.

"We know why they sent us on a fool's errand to Sam's Club on a Sunday," he said as they backed out of the driveway. "Same place as before?" he said.

"Yes," Nancy said, blinking back tears.

"Why are you crying?" Steve said, grasping his wife's hand.

"They are so much in love," Nancy said. "I'm just so happy."

Steve pulled into the parking lot of the donut shop and took his wife in his arms, kissing her tears away. 'I know, sweetness, I know," he said.

THE END

If you enjoyed

Cabin Fever

Check out the first book in the series

Double Dare

Turn the page for a preview

Chapter 1

Liz Renfew's face hurt from stretching it into a phony smile. How could she hate another human being to the depths of her soul the way she hated Luke Reddington? She felt this way even though they stood in a church together as godparents to her best friend Amy and Luke's best friend Gray's twins, Jordan and Jack.

She kept her eyes on Jordan, who she held in her arms. She couldn't, wouldn't look at Luke. She thought he was hot, even though she loathed him with every fiber of her being.

And he was her husband.

He'd married her after she had dared him to in Las Vegas. And the worm wouldn't sign the divorce papers.

Damn Amy for leaving her alone with him and riding off with Gray into the desert moonlight. Her plan was to give Amy a wild girl's night and convince her not to marry Gray. He had left dear, sweet Amy standing at the altar just months before in a whacked-up retaliation for Amy breaking up with his buddy Smitty.

Smitty died soon after—on patrol in Afghanistan, where he, Gray, and Luke were stationed. He had made his relationship with Amy sound much more serious that it was. Amy still had her V-card till she seduced Gray a week before the morning he'd jilted her. And Luke helped him rip Amy's heart out. He drove the getaway car.

Then Luke had the nerve to show up at Amy's place a couple months later to beg Amy to go to Gray, who'd gone off the rails, and talk to him. Amy had caved and gone to him, because she blamed herself for what she believed to be her part in Smitty's death—breaking up with him right before went on his last, fatal patrol, which Amy believed made him reckless or careless. Gray asked her for another chance.

And Amy, sweet, loving Amy, did—but not after making him sweat it out.

Liz looked at Amy. She was radiant with her love for

Gray and her babies. And Liz had to admit Gray was crazy in love with Amy.

He'd even given her the chance to dump his ass in front of the minister and their family and friends in Vegas like he did to her, but she didn't.

Liz glared at Luke. He pursed his mouth into a kiss.

She should have shot him when he showed up at Amy's place that day. Her brothers and dad were sheriffs in Emmett County where Amy used to live, which was in Petoskey, near Lake Michigan. Liz had her twenty-two-caliber pistol in her purse and her permit to carry it. Her brothers and dad had taught her how to shoot after her disastrous senior prom night.

Jordan started fussing. She handed the baby to Amy's mom Nancy and was surprised that she immediately missed the smell and feel of the infant in her arms. Luke relinquished Jack to Steve, Amy's dad, and stood next to her. He smelled woodsy.

"How is my darling wife?"

"Shut up. Someone will hear."

"Ashamed of me, baby cakes?"

"Yes. Just sign the damned divorce papers." She flashed Amy a big, fake smile. She hadn't told Amy about that night in Vegas. There never seemed to be a good time.

Then Amy had been a smitten newlywed, then pregnant, then sleep-deprived. Amy was looking at them now and frowning.

Why wouldn't he sign the damned papers?

Liz had gotten drunk that night and dared him to marry her.

And he did, although she passed out cold in their hotel room promptly after the ceremony, so nothing had happened.

And now she could only bring herself to release when she thought of him.

⌘

Her scent hit him, vanilla and some spice he couldn't name, and he went instantly hard. Fuck. He wasn't signing those damned divorce papers. Not until she gave them a chance. Amy and Gray were with her parents, talking to the priest, so he took hold of his wife's waist and hustled her into a small alcove, keeping her back to him. She'd worn her hair down, and he remembered it spread out on the pillow on their wedding night.

"I'll sign your damned divorce decree, but I have a condition," he whispered in her ear.

She tried to turn to face him, but he tightened his hold on her waist so she wouldn't see his obvious erection.

"Spend one night with me—sober."

"That makes zero sense. We didn't consummate it. It's cut and dried."

"Take it or leave it." He nuzzled her neck.

She stood as still as the statue of the Blessed Virgin in the alcove.

Amy called her name, and she wrenched herself away from him. "All right. I agree. I just want this over with."

She stared into his eyes. He lifted a strand of her hair.

"Stop that, someone will see."

He nuzzled her neck again. "When, baby cakes?"

Her brown eyes blazed gold. "Stop calling me that. The sooner, the better."

"Mmmm." He bit down on her neck. "So eager."

"Hey?" Amy stood at the entrance to the alcove, juggling Jordan and a diaper bag. Her mouth gaped open.

"Later," he said.

∽∾∽

Luke stroked Jordan's bonnet as he walked away.

"Holy hell," Amy said.

"That's so wrong, saying it here," Liz said.

Amy handed her the diaper bag. "Do you want to talk about it?"

"Later."

Liz drove back to Amy and Gray's condo and helped with the babies during brunch. Luke held Jack for a time. Watching him with the infant did odd things to her chest and stomach. Needing to focus on something else, she handed Jordan to Amy's mom and started to clean up the dishes.

Her heart thudded in her chest when Luke joined her in the kitchen and handed her dishes to rinse. She clenched her jaw.

They worked well together. What was up with that?

"I know, right?"

He flashed her a shit-eating grin. She fought the urge to grin back. She was so not doing this. He was a heartless jerk, just like that asshole on prom night.

She scowled.

He tapped the tip of her nose. "You look so cute when you scrunch your face up like that."

"Just thinking about Amy's face when you and Gray left her standing alone at the altar. I have a thing about jerks who hurt innocent people."

He frowned, filled the sink with soapy water, and started washing the pots, pans, and casseroles. "Smitty was full of shit. I didn't know that then. Gray told me after."

Just then, Gray hauled a giggling Amy past the kitchen and up the stairs.

"Don't worry, we've got this." Luke's lips quirked into a smile. "He's crazy in love with her, Liz, I mean bat shit crazy. You didn't see him after he left her. It nearly killed him."

She saw a speck of food on the casserole dish that Luke had just washed and dumped it back in the water, which pissed him off.

Good.

He sighed. "I didn't know that Smitty lied. Gray didn't tell me until after. Hell of it is, I still miss the asshole." He rewashed the casserole and set it in the drainer. "Amy seems to be happy, wouldn't you say?"

She picked up the casserole, which was spotless, and dropped it back in the dishwater.

"That was clean, baby cakes."

"Nu-uh," she said.

He took the clean casserole out of the dish water and sloshed soapy water down the front of her white, lacy blouse.

He smirked. "Oh, sorry."

He rinsed the dish off and set it in the drainer. She took it out, dunked it in the soapy water, and dumped it over his head.

"You'll pay for that baby cakes."

She dunked the dish in the water again and poured it down the front of his pants. "Do. Not. Call. Me. That."

Holy hell. His erection was clearly visible. He followed her stare and laughed. "What do you expect?" He hauled her into his arms like a limp doll.

What was wrong with her? Why did he smell so wonderful?

He traced the outline of her lips with his tongue while he pulled her hard against him.

Did he have any fat at all on his lean, hard frame?

"I'll scream," she said, although she bit back a sigh when his hands moved to her back side to lift her onto the kitchen counter. He wrapped her legs around his waist.

"You will scream my name when I make you come."

He plundered her mouth, and his hand slipped under her skirt then under her thong to her slit. She was wet, damn it, and he groaned. He plunged his tongue in and out as he worked his finger inside her. She did scream, but the noise was muffled by his mouth.

Breathing hard, she stared into his impossibly blue eyes. They were triumphant but tender. He rested his damp forehead on hers.

"My darling wife," he said, smiling.

"Is everything okay?" Amy's mom stood in the doorway. "The babies are down. Oh—"she said, scurrying away.

Liz let loose a string of expletives. She pushed away from him and off the kitchen counter.

Fuck him. Fuck Gray. "And fuck Amy."

He took hold of her shoulders. His blue eyes had gone silver, and a muscle near his mouth twitched. He was angry. "Fuck Amy?" he said.

Shit, had she said the last part out loud?

"There's plenty of dishwater here to wash out that mouth of yours." His hands moved to her waist. "I do not like those words on your beautiful lips."

"Tough shit."

He backed her up against the sink, dipped his hand in the dishwater, and covered her mouth with it. "They are happy, Liz. You have to see that. Even though you and I did our best to fuck that up."

She bit his hand hard.

"Fuck."

"So you're allowed to say fuck, and I'm not. Fuck that. And I did not try to fuck it up."

She smiled. She'd said fuck three times in twenty seconds.

"You're pissed that Amy gave him another chance. Why?"

He left her and didn't wait for an answer.

About the Author

Tara Eldana is an award-winning staff writer for a weekly community newspaper chain in metro Detroit. She became hooked on romance fiction when her eleventh grade English teacher rejected the book report she wrote, saying the book was much too easy for her, and insisted she read and report on Daphne du Maurier's *Rebecca*. Eldana had read Margaret Mitchell's *Gone with the Wind* that previous summer.

Eldana took a long road through J-school, graduating from Oakland University in Rochester, Michigan in '95, just shy of twenty years after she finished high school, raising a couple kids, working part-time, and doing her homework while her husband and kids watched TV. Still, she found time to read what her kids called her "mush books."

Eldana loves the romance genre and loves letting her characters take control of their stories. She is a member of the Greater Detroit Romance Writers of America.

Visit her at taraeldana.com, on Facebook, Instagram or Twitter. She loves to hear from her readers.

www.ingramcontent.com/pod-product-compliance
Lightning Source LLC
Chambersburg PA
CBHW071008120726
47910CB00004B/1440